DAY THE WIND CHANGED

A SHORT STORY

ALEXANDRIA BLAELOCK

Also by Alexandria Blaelock

SHORT STORY COLLECTIONS
The Histories of Hayward Hall
Lovelorn, Lovestruck and Love at First Sight
Common or Garden Variety Heroes
Case Files of the Wilkinson Detective Agency
Unavoidable Fates
Christmas Travesties
Five Faces of Felicia Clarke
Little Place Called Home
Security Directorate Dossiers v. 1.
Security Directorate Dossiers v. 2.

FICTION
That Love Nonsense
Taipan vs Brown
The Ghost and Ms Cox
Friends Like That
Weaving the Wildwood
Wolf vs Orb

MS BLAELOCK'S BOOKS
Stress Free Dinner Parties
Signature Wardrobe Planning
Holistic Personal Finance
Minimally Viable Housekeeping
Planning a Life Worth Living

PICTURE BOOKS
Australia Felix

A SELECTION OF AVAILABLE SHORT STORIES
Alma's Grace
Blood and Bloody Profanity
Cancelled by the Cartel
Dingo Hunting
Dream House
Honoris Virilis Respectu
Mince Pie Mystery
Remains of Christmas
Shining Star
Susan and the Gangster
The Day the Schedule Broke
The Trembling Tower

DAY THE WIND CHANGED

A SHORT STORY

ALEXANDRIA BLAELOCK

BlueMere Books

MELBOURNE, AUSTRALIA

For permission requests, please contact
enquiries@bluemerebooks.com.

Ordering Information:
Discounts are available on quantity purchases. For details, contact orders@bluemerebooks.com.

Day the Wind Changed/Alexandria Blaelock
paperback ISBN: 978-1-923083-20-2
digital ISBN: 978-1-923083-21-9

Book Layout © BookDesignTemplates.com
Cover Art © grandfailure/depositphotos

DAY THE WIND CHANGED

Souta shoved a grape in her mouth, and her hands in her pockets as she leaned against the wooden door frame to watch the clouds forming over the hills.

A warm wind pushed an advance guard of black shadows racing across the land, reaching the house moments before it carried in the sound of birds and the smell of rain.

She sighed.

Some days, life was just so much the same that she longed to move away. To live in a different village, meet different people, and see different things.

Mother grunted from the back room, but Souta stayed still. She didn't care what the old woman wanted. The old cow was the only thing holding her in this place.

One day she'd die, and Souta would be free to follow the wind to the ends of the earth, or wherever else she pleased.

The temptation to walk out the back of the house and climb the path up and over the hills was so strong she stepped over the sill.

But Mother yelled something, and the force of duty sent Souta to see what she wanted.

Mother is a strange word, isn't it? At its most basic, it refers to the woman who gave birth to you or the woman who cares for you.

But Mother was neither of those things.

Souta's birth parents were both dead, and someone somewhere had sent her to foster with Mother.

Who was happy to accept a small payment to cover Souta's costs, but not spend any of it on her.

If anything, Souta was the giver of care, always had been.

Aside from cooking, cleaning and providing clean clothes, she'd been sent out into the fields of a neighbour to earn money almost as soon as she'd arrived.

None of which she was supposed to keep.

Though, of course, she'd managed to hide a coin here and there; a little something to save and spend on herself in some other place, at some time in the future.

She didn't doubt that despite her long years of caring for Mother, there'd be nothing for her when the woman died.

Not even the right to live in this ramshackle shack.

Souta knew she wasn't pretty or clever, but she sure wasn't stupid.

And some time couldn't come soon enough.

When Souta arrived at Mother's room, the old woman was lying stiff and contorted on her pallet on the floor.

Maybe she was right when she said you shouldn't scowl in case the wind changed, and you stayed that way.

"Mother," Souta cried and rushed to the pallet to shake her.

There was no response, so Souta attempted to unfold her, but the body was more rigid than the rickety table they ate off.

Souta put a finger under the woman's nose, but couldn't feel a whisper of breath. With the greatest of reluctance, she lay two fingers under the jaw, but couldn't feel a pulse.

It seemed that some time had finally come.

And not being stupid, she knew the full blame for Mother's death would be laid on her, whether by magic, or poison, or some other cause.

The first few drops of rain pelted down on the roof, granting Souta a little time to prepare.

Not that she thought anyone would visit, but it wouldn't hurt to get ready.

Or to make sure she was well away before anyone did.

First, she folded some clothes and all the cash she could find into a blanket.

As she was searching for the cash, she found some jewellery, so she folded that into the pack along with a kitchen knife and a basic sewing kit.

Added a large, tatty umbrella for shelter, and she was ready to be on her way.

Now.

While Souta knew Mother had died naturally, she needed to make sure anyone who found her that way wouldn't need much convincing to think the same.

The wind and rain were starting to increase, lightning cracked, and thunder boomed shaking the house. A piece of tin from the roof creaked and groaned as the wind lifted and dropped it.

Rain slipped through the gap.

Was it possible the monsoon could pull the house down?

Was there anything she could do to encourage it?

Like open all the doors and windows to let the wind do its worse?

Or would it be better to open just the ones on the valley side in the hope they'd blow out the ones on the other?

While the rain was still heavy enough to cover the noise, she threw all the house's contents around.

Partly to make the place look wind affected, and partly so there were plenty of loose items for the wind to play with.

Then, with the wind's help, she threw the front door open so hard it caught and stuck.

And couldn't be shut without a lot of effort.

Which she wasn't going to make.

It was almost full dark when she picked up her pack to leave, through true night was still some hours away.

She opened the umbrella, pulled it close to her head and let the wind push her up the hill.

Walked for a while, and just before she reached the crest, she turned to look back.

A sheet of lightning illuminated the valley just long enough to see a tree fall onto the house, smashing it to pieces and start sliding down the hill into the valley.

She couldn't believe her luck.

If the rain was still falling, it was more likely the village would assume she'd been cut into tiny pieces by the detritus and washed away.

Regardless of what they thought, she was fairly confident they wouldn't come looking for her, and that her life was just now beginning.

And a new life needed a new name.

«« • »»

Souta's second piece of luck, though she didn't realise that's what it was, came on a day the wind changed as well.

Not long after she'd escaped the village.

She was walking down a road lined with tall trees in the rain. Her wet, squelching sandals provided a steady beat for the music of the rain falling on the surprisingly durable umbrella.

It was a warm day, and despite her wet feet, she felt unusually light and free.

She wasn't entirely sure what she was feeling, but she thought it might be happiness.

And because she was puzzling through her feelings, she wasn't really looking where she was going.

She only saw the old woman, sheltering under a tree on a pile of her possessions, because she was startled by a movement seen from the corner of her eye.

"Grandmother," she called, "are you okay?"

The old woman laughed, "I'm well thank you. I'm just waiting for the rain to stop so I can go on my way."

"Have you been waiting long?"

"I don't know. You know how it is with these Summer storms."

"Of course Grandmother. But you look tired, can I offer you something to eat and drink?"

"That's very kind, but I assure you I'm fine."

"I guess it'd be hard to get a fire going in this rain anyway."

And at that very moment, the rain stopped falling on them, and they paused for a moment to watch the storm's trailing edge travelling away from them.

The old woman sneezed.

"My goodness Grandmother," said Souta, "you're soaked, let me at least dry your hair."

She unwrapped her pack, pulled out a clean sarong, and gently patted down the old woman's head.

"That's much better, thank you," she said before sneezing again.

"I heard there's a Monastery away down the road that has a doctor, shall I take you there?"

"Ah yes, the Temple of Wind. I've heard of it, but I don't think I need a doctor.

"Still it's on my way, and I expect if we stop in, they'll have some hot tea to share."

The old woman stood and started collecting her things together until she looked like a shrivelled up old, and overburdened donkey.

"Grandmother, you can't carry all that, let me take some for you."

"No, no, there's no need," and tried unsuccessfully to stand up.

"I think you can see there is some need Grandmother. Please let me help."

"All right then," shesaid, and dropped every thing back to the ground. "Perhaps you could take the sewing machine box."

Souta picked up the box.

"Perhaps that blue stripy bag as well."

Souta picked up the bag.

"Could you manage the red bag do you think?"

Souta picked up the red bag.

"What about the white one?

And before too long, Souta was holding all the old woman's things. Though it seemed to her, she was holding more than had been on the ground in the first place.

"That looks heavy child, will you be all right."

Souta adjusted the load a little, "of course Grandmother, I don't know how you managed all of this."

And she really didn't.

"Perhaps you'd let me carry your bag?"

It seemed a little ridiculous, but somehow necessary to surrender her small pack.

"Thank you Grandmother, if you're sure you can manage?"

"I'll be fine child."

And somehow, Souta was too.

As Grandmother settled the pack on her shoulders, Souta felt as though an even greater load had been removed from her own.

"Then, shall we go Grandmother?"

The old woman nodded her assent and they started their journey along the road.

It wasn't too much later they joined a throng of worshippers walking down the broad avenue to the temple.

Souta's steps slowed as she tried to take them all in.

She'd never seen so many people in one place, more even than lived in the whole village.

The more she looked, the more she saw.

And the more she saw, the more afraid she became.

Who knew there were even that many people in the world?

Who was she to think she was anyone special?

She didn't realise she'd stopped walking until Grandmother patted her arm, "come along child, there's room in this place for all, no matter how deserving."

Souta shook herself and started walking again, this time ignoring the people and focusing on the beautiful, landscaped gardens and the sweet scent of the fiery orange flowers.

It would be wonderful to stay here. Maybe she'd enjoy working in the Monastery fields if she could look back at the gardens.

Or maybe they'd let her cultivate the flowers instead of the food.

Grandmother sneezed again.

Souta remembered that getting a doctor to see Grandmother was the reason they'd come there and started looking for something that would indicate where he was.

But Grandmother saw the tea house first and headed in that direction.

Souta could only follow.

They made themselves comfortable, sitting in the queue and settling their bags and boxes around them.

It didn't take as long as Souta expected for the doctor to arrive, followed by a group of acolytes.

She was grateful she didn't need to worry about that anymore.

He asked Grandmother some questions, looked in her eyes and felt her neck. Then he barked a word at the acolytes, and one broke away at a run.

And then he did the same to her, despite her protests that she was fine.

The doctor said some things about energy and balance she didn't understand, but she thought he probably knew best, and let him look in her eyes and feel her neck as well.

He shouted a different word, and another acolyte ran off.

Not much later, the acolytes came back with a big mug of tea each. Souta found hers citrus scented with a vaguely floral taste. And as she drank, it seemed that there was some kind of change within her.

A sort of lightness and brightness that hadn't been there before.

"How's your tea child?"

"It's delicious Grandmother, would you like a taste?"

"No thank you my dear, that tea is made from the ingredients you need right now, it won't do me any good.

"But I am suddenly very tired. Could you watch me while I take a nap?"

"Of course Grandmother." Souta set her tea aside, unrolled her pack and laid it out like a bag for Grandmother to lie in.

"Do you know child; I think you're very lucky."

Souta snorted, "what makes you think that Grandmother?"

"Here you are, happy and healthy, with no obligations so pressing you can't spend a little time with an old lady you don't know."

"I suppose when you put it that way, I am quite lucky. Though I haven't always been that way."

"Where I come from... the word for someone lucky like you is Kiaria..."

Souta drank some more tea and turned the word over in her mouth as Grandmother snored gently beside her.

"Kiaria."

It sounded light and bright, just like the tea made her feel.

"Kiaria."

It was easy to say, flowing off her tongue like water and through her ears like a gentle breeze.

It was a good name.

She drank the last of her tea, and despite her best intentions, lulled by the mid-afternoon warmth, fell asleep by Grandmother's side.

《《 • 》》

When she woke, she was nestled in the pile of Grandmother's things. Panicked, she sat up but found no sign of Grandmother or her own small pack.

"Grandmother," she called out before springing to her feet and looking further afield.

"Grandmother?"

Aside from the stack of her belongings, there was nothing to suggest the old woman had ever been there.

She turned to the woman next to her in the queue, "excuse me, did you see where Grandmother went?"

"Grandmother? What Grandmother? You've been alone here all day."

"Nonsense, these are all her things! Now, where is she?"

"Don't be ridiculous girl, I saw you come in carrying all those things."

"But the doctor saw her, she had tea!"

The woman put her fists on her hips, "I've been here all day, and I didn't see you with anyone."

The woman's raised voice drew the attention of an acolyte who hurried over.

"Did you see Grandmother," she asked him.

"I did not, it is as this woman said. You were alone all day."

Kiaria massaged her temples, "but she was here. I saw her. These are her things..."

The acolyte put a hand on her shoulder, "perhaps you should speak with my Master."

He helped her gather all Grandmother's belongings before leading her down a garden path, through a gate, and into a small, paved courtyard.

He stacked Grandmother's things in a pile in the corner.

"Please wait here," he said, as he left.

She sat on a rock shaped into a block, folded her hands in her lap, and took a deep breath in to sigh out.

As she inhaled the still air of the courtyard, it weighed heavily in her chest.

Not in a bad, suffocating way, but as if the centuries of quiet, serene meditation were soaking into her body.

Grounding her and calming her fears for Grandmother.

She closed her eyes to try and understand the feeling better, and when she opened them, she was facing a wizened old man in a plain red robe.

She waited for the Master to speak.

After a little while, he said, "The woman you know as Grandmother is a wind spirit."

She frowned but waited for the Master to continue.

"These things," he gestured at the stack, "are her gifts to you.

"Have you made an offering to her?"

Kiaria lowered her eyes, "Um, well, the wind took the house I was living in. And Grandmother took my things. Is that what you mean?"

After a pause, Master said, "that could be it. Was there anything else?"

She squirmed on the rock for a moment, then decided to trust him.

"Mother died in the storm that took the house. Was that maybe my first offering, or my first gift?"

Master thought for a moment, "that depends on her relationship with the wind, and that is not for us to know.

"The wind gives, and the wind takes away. All you need to do is love and respect the wind."

Kiaria hadn't thought she could feel any lighter, yet she did.

"Thank you Master."

He gestured to the room behind him, "you may stay in this guest room tonight, but tomorrow, you must go where the wind sends you."

《《 • 》》

Kiaria smiled at the woman, "thank you," she said, walking around the shop counter to hand her the crisp white paper bag containing her new dress. "I hope this dress brings you a lot of joy."

"Thank you! I'm sure it will."

Working in her own dress shop was much nicer than working in fields, whether they be food or flowers.

It didn't matter how rude the customers were, it was always more pleasant to wear pretty dresses, in a neat and clean shop than grub about in a field.

Especially a shop with racks of brightly coloured clothes hanging on the walls, waving gently in the soft swirl of air created by the overhead fans.

Now and again she'd run her hands along the racks enjoying the smooth, soft textures against her palms.

Or sometimes, push her face in between them to enjoy their clean, dry smell.

Arrange and rearrange them into different colour combinations.

Or just lean on the wall, close her eyes, and listen to the music she played for company.

She wouldn't be sad if she never saw never-ending rows and rows of plants to be weeded.

Or miss the smell of damp dirt and animal shit. The risk of standing in it. The sound of other field workers mouth breathing and complaining.

Some might say it was all luck - being in the right place at the right time.

But none of it would have happened if the wind hadn't changed and allowed her to escape the village in the first place.

If she hadn't left when she did, she wouldn't have been there when luck came looking to grant someone's wishes.

But that first piece of luck had been her own - choosing to leave, not waiting around to see what the village would do with her.

Or to her.

It was something she often wanted to say to the unhappy, whiny, pretty women who gossiped in her shop while she fitted their dresses.

Luck was something you made yourself.

As she showed her last customer the door, she dimmed the lights, turned off the fan, and locked the door.

She patted the sewing machine before climbing the stairs to her tiny apartment, where all the windows were always open a crack.

She took a glass of wine and a snack onto the balcony, jammed with wheels, flags and chimes for the wind to play with.

Tipped out a little wine and threw a few crumbs for the wind to take before taking hers.

Life was perfect.

She lived alone.

There were no angry, argumentative women demanding gratitude and respect where none was deserved.

Nothing missing from this pleasant life, in this neat shop, with her cosy apartment.

Except maybe a husband.

Someone to snuggle and share her problems with.

Someone to take care of her, as she took care of him.

The wind picked up a little, setting the chimes jangling.

Kiaria looked up into the setting sun and saw no sign of a storm coming.

But there was a strange smell in the air.

Not like you get with a fire, and not like you get before a storm.

Something electric, a bit like lightning.

And yet strangely familiar.

The hair on her arms stood on end.

Unsettling.

She left her food and drink on the balcony, and trotted downstairs to the shop.

Paused, feeling the shop around her.

It looked the same, its peace undisturbed by unusual sounds or smells.

Nothing strange at all.

Whatever it was, wasn't in the shop.

She unlocked the door, and stepped outside, into the orange-tinted light.

It was here, this unsettling thing, whatever it was.

She waited, turning her head from side to side, for it to show itself.

The wind picked up again, sighing gently and blowing bits of rubbish in eddies around the lamp posts.

And as she watched, a shadow detached itself from one of the buildings and staggered into the street.

It was a man, bent over, hands clasped to his abdomen.

She ran to help him.

Even bent over, he was tall. And his arms, as she reached out to grab him, were hard and lumpy with muscle.

He raised his head to look at her, revealing preternaturally shining blue eyes.

For a moment, she was afraid and pulled back, but the wind pushed her towards him.

Perhaps he was the wind's third gift. Someone to care for.

She pulled him into the shop and closed the door.

THE END

As a small token of my thanks for reading...

Please enjoy one time 10% off everything
(excluding shipping)

at alexandriablaelock.com

with the code kiariaten.

Turn the page for some ideas where to use it,

Please consider The Ghost and Ms Cox

Life interrupted

To say the letter was a surprise was an understatement. It arrived addressed to Miss Finlay Cox, which made the contents even more extraordinary.

Orphan Finn Cox inherits a cottage. Thinks it holds the key to her origins. Of course she takes a look. Who wouldn't?

But when she gets there, she gets more than she bargained for.

Is it friend, family or foe?

Weaving the Wildwood

All she wants is a place of her own.

When Alison Porter finds a tiny cottage for sale, she thinks her dreams have come true. Inside virgin bushland, "Crow Cottage" sits on the smallest parcel of cleared land.

It's old. It's run down. It's keeping a secret.

Stumbling through a mysterious portal in the garden, she finds herself in a place of mystery and intrigue. As the past, present and future collide, she must unravel the secret, for only then can she reweave the tapestry of time.

If you love a story of twists and turns, where nothing is what it seems, grab Weaving the Wildwood today.

The Histories of Hayward Hall

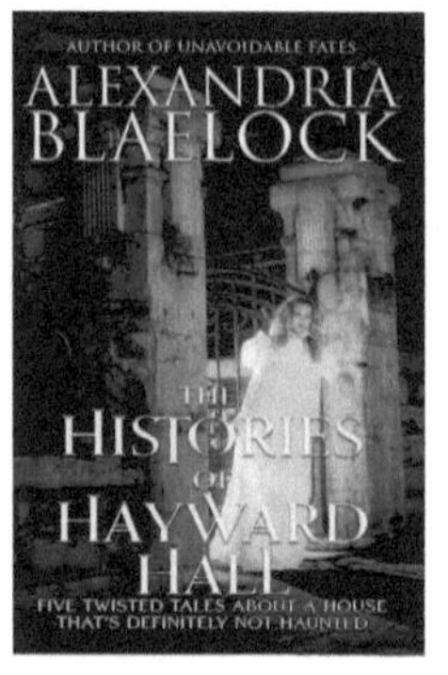

Meet Morag Clementine. The new housekeeper at historic Hayward Hall.

Her practical and capable attitude usually keeps her out of trouble.

bove all, her no-nonsense, get it done approach. And her get in the middle of the scrum outlook. Just as well, because Hayward Hall needs someone like her.

In this genre-spanning collection of original stories, Morag finds herself ensnared in the History of Hayward Hall...

No ordinary housekeeper, can Morag save the house, one century at a time?

Little Place Called Home

Home is where the heart is

You can struggle to find the place you call home. It's not a place, it's a feeling.

You'll know it when you find it.

This collection of short stories explores our search for a place we can call home.

Short, sweet and relatable, these stories will make you homesick for places you've never been.

*Perhaps you'll carry your new books in
one of these bags*

*And enjoy them while you're drinking
from one of these mugs*

ABOUT THE AUTHOR

Australian author Alexandria Blaelock writes mostly fantasy and mystery.

She's appeared in the Stringybark Anthology *Crowd Surfing, Pulphouse Fiction Magazine,* and *Ellery Queen's Mystery Magazine.*

She's also written five self-help books applying business techniques to personal matters like getting dressed, tidying up, and feeding friends.

When not exploring parallel universes, she talks to animals, indulges in K-dramas, and sips Campari. She lives in the Dandenongs, where she relishes the sound of birdsong, the scent of gum leaves and the sun on her face.

Discover more at https://alexandriablaelock.com.